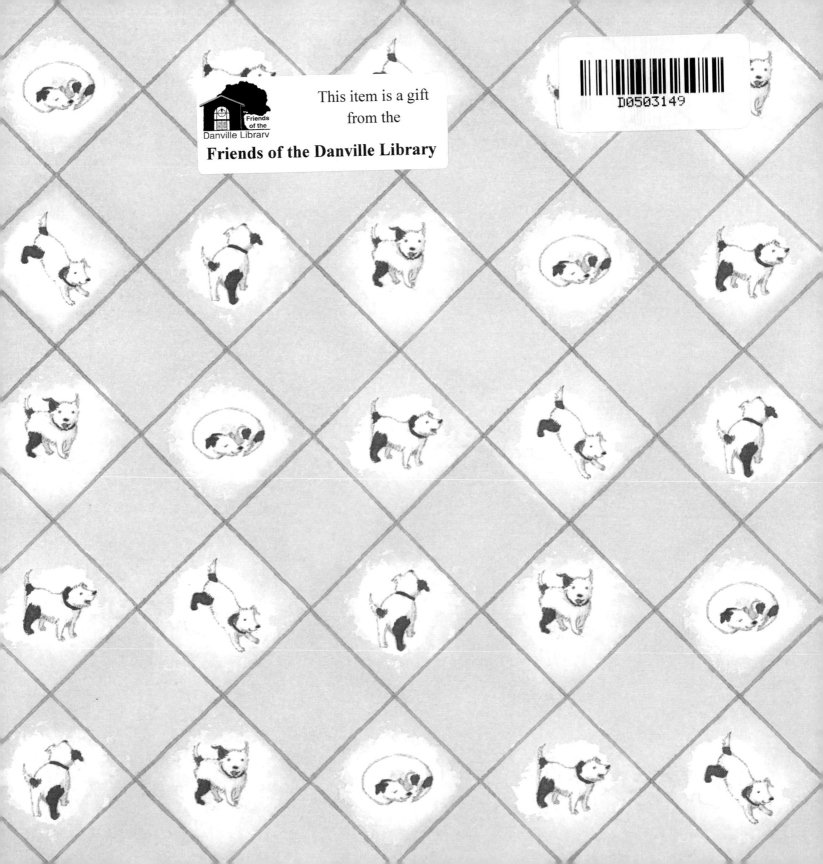

Madame Martine
Breaks the Rules

SARAH S. BRANNEN

ALBERT WHITMAN & COMPANY
CHICAGO, ILLINOIS

FOR ALEXA SCHULZ REBER,
A BRILLIANT ARTIST WHO ATE
CHOCOLATE IN THE LOUVRE WITH ME

AND WITH THANKS TO
MARNI TYSON GALLAGHER

Library of Congress Cataloging-in-Publication
data is on file with the publisher.

Text and pictures copyright © 2015 Sarah S. Brannen
Published in 2015 by Albert Whitman & Company
ISBN 978-0-8075-4907-0

Printed in China
10 9 8 7 6 5 4 3 2 1 HH 20 19 18 17 16 15

Design by Jordan Kost

For more information about Albert Whitman & Company,
visit our web site at www.albertwhitman.com.

Madame Martine and her dog, Max, lived in
a tall, narrow apartment building in the city of Paris.
They did everything together.

Every day Madame Martine and Max
had breakfast in the same café before
they did their shopping. Sometimes their
friend Louis sat with them.

"Time to go to work," said Louis. He gave Max his usual biscuit and then asked his usual question. "Would you like to visit me at the museum today?"

Louis had been a guard at the Louvre Museum for fifty years. Madame Martine never went to the museum.

"Oh no," said Madame Martine. "It's so crowded, and they don't allow dogs."

"For you and Max, we might break the rules," said Louis.

Madame Martine was shocked. "We would never ask you to do that!" she said.

Madame Martine and Max always tried new things on Saturdays.

That Saturday, they rode the Métro to the Palais Royale stop.

They set off up the street, looking for something new to do.

Suddenly Max leaped forward and pulled his leash out of Madame Martine's hand.

"Max!" cried Madame Martine.

Max was bounding up the street, following a familiar figure. Louis turned around in surprise. Max sat in front of him and wagged his tail.

"Oh, have you decided to visit the museum?" asked Louis.

"We can't!" said Madame Martine. "Dogs are not allowed."

"There might be a way—" began Louis.

"Where is Max?" yelled Madame Martine.

"*Mon dieu,*" said Louis. He and Madame Martine ran through the employee entrance as Max vanished down a hallway.

"A dog!" shouted someone.

"Get it!" yelled someone else.

"Oh no," moaned Madame Martine.

Madame Martine and Louis ran toward the yelling. They turned a corner and saw Max rushing back at them. Madame Martine grabbed his leash.

"Quick!" said Madame Martine. She picked Max up and darted into a broom closet.

"*Tiens!*" said Louis. He jumped into the closet too.

Madame Martine peeked out and saw two guards running past.

"*Alors,*" said Louis, mopping his brow. "Since you're here now, would you like a little tour?"

"No!" said Madame Martine. "We must get out of here!"

"Too bad," said Louis. He winked at Max.

"Come with me. I know every inch of this place."

They scurried through a hall of statues.

"This, for instance, is a Lamassu statue,

from Assyria..."

"Shhh!" said Madame Martine.

"They'll hear you!"

"Ah, look! It's Diana, goddess of the hunt," said Louis.

"Don't move!" said Madame Martine. "I see the guards."

A tourist saw Max and giggled.

They ran up a flight of stairs past paintings, statues, and hundreds of tourists. Madame Martine felt lost amid all the art. Max nuzzled her cheek.

"Are we almost out of here?" asked Madame Martine.

"Nearly," said Louis. "But we must say hello to Mona Lisa first."

"Ohhh," whispered Madame Martine. "She is more beautiful than I ever imagined."

"There they are!" shouted a guard.

Madame Martine, Louis,
and Max ran toward the exit.
The guards ran after them.
"Louis, stop!" shouted
the guards.

Madame Martine turned and looked at the guards with dismay.

A guard shook Louis's hand and said, "Aren't you going to introduce us to your friends?"

"I know dogs aren't allowed," said Madame Martine. "I am sorry I broke your rules!"

"For a friend of Louis, we can bend the rules," said the guard.

Madame Martine sighed with relief. Max wagged his tail.

"I hope you enjoyed your visit," said Louis.

"It was much more exciting than I expected," said Madame Martine. "Maybe we can go somewhere else next Saturday. Somewhere dogs are permitted."

"That sounds delightful," said Louis.

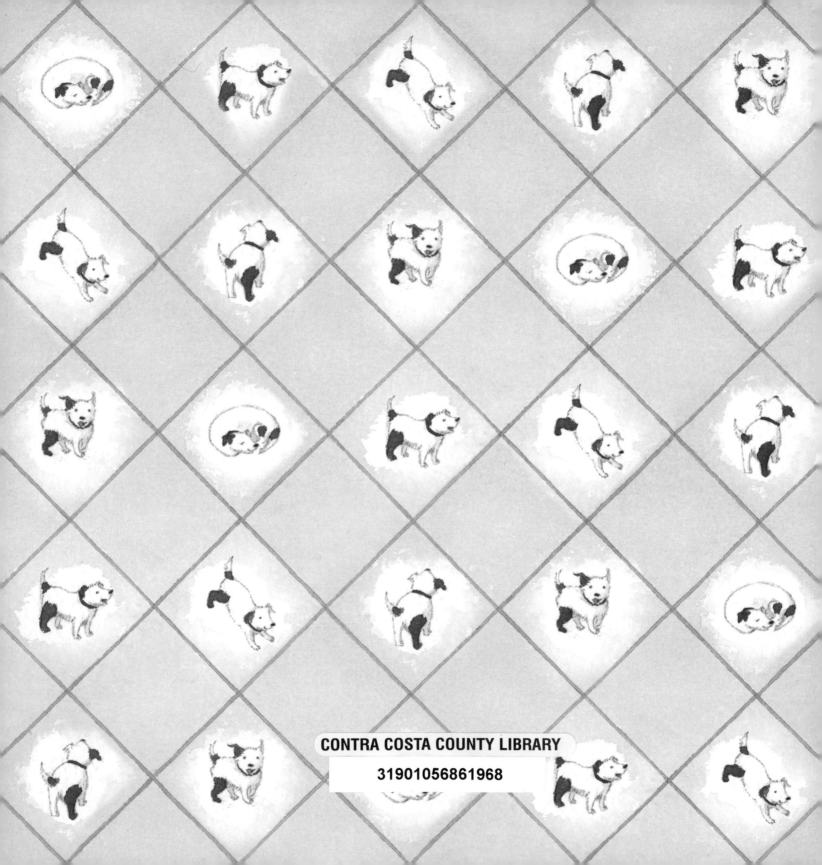